Key Lardo

Chet Gecko Mysteries

The Chameleon Wore Chartreuse
The Mystery of Mr. Nice
Farewell, My Lunchbag
The Big Nap
The Hamster of the Baskervilles
This Gum for Hire
The Malted Falcon
Trouble Is My Beeswax
Give My Regrets to Broadway
Murder, My Tweet
The Possum Always Rings Twice
Key Lardo

And don't miss
Chet Gecko's Detective Handbook (and Cookbook):
Tips for Private Eyes and Snack Food Lovers

Key Lardo

FROM THE TATTERED CASEBOOK OF

CHET GECKO
PRIVATE EYE

Bruce Hale

HARCOURT, INC.

Orlando • Austin • New York • San Diego • Toronto • London

www.HarcourtBooks.com

Library of Congress Cataloging-in-Publication Data
Hale, Bruce.
Key Lardo/Bruce Hale.
p. cm.
Summary: When the new penguin at school turns out to be a private eye,
Chet Gecko confronts not only a devious sparrow but also his own jealousy.
[1. Jealousy—Fiction. 2. Geckos—Fiction. 3. Penguins—Fiction.
4. Schools—Fiction. 5. Mystery and detective stories.
6. Humorous stories.] I. Title.
PZ7.H1295Key 2006
[Fic]—dc22 2006006026
ISBN-13: 978-0-15-205074-0 ISBN-10: 0-15-205074-4

Text set in Bembo
Display type set in Elroy
Designed by April Ward

First edition
A C E G H F D B

Printed in the United States of America

To that swell and swingin' combo, the Collins Clan

A private message from the private eye . . .

Without mysteries, life would be slower than two slugs waltzing (but not quite as slimy). Luckily for me, life is full of mysteries.

Like, if peanut butter cookies are made from peanuts, what are Girl Scout cookies made of? If athletes get athlete's foot, do rocket scientists get mistletoe? And if swimming is so good for your shape, why do whales look the way they do?

Even if I weren't Chet Gecko, Emerson Hicky Elementary's top lizard detective, I'd be a mystery lover. But in my time, I've learned that some mysteries come with a steep price.

Working this one case, I nearly lost my detective mojo—and to a guy so dim, he'd probably play goalie for the darts team. True, he was only a cog in a larger conspiracy. But this big buttinsky made my life more uncomfortable than a porcupine's embrace.

My reputation took a nosedive. And I nearly followed it—straight into the slammer. Fighting back with all my moxie, I bent the rules, blundered into blind alleys, and stepped on more than a few toes.

Was I right? Was I wrong? I'll tell you this: I made my share of mistakes. But I believe that if you can't laugh at yourself... make fun of someone else.

1

Penguin Pal

It all started with a muffin. And despite my best intentions, it went downhill from there, quicker than a walrus on roller skates.

Wednesday is Italian Day in the cafeteria. On this particular Wednesday, Mrs. Bagoong and her cooks had worked their usual magic—spaghetti with millipede meatballs, eggplant à la fungus gnat, and honey-glazed Madagascan Hissing Cockroach muffins.

The muffins set off a taste explosion that had my tongue dancing the Madagascan Mambo (or whatever kind of hoofing they do over there).

I pushed back from the table and headed over to score another one. Most kids don't get to have seconds.

But I'm not most kids.

Bellying up to the lunch counter, I could tell that the baked goodies had been a hit. All had vanished but one.

And that one had Chet Gecko's name on it.

"Hey, Brown Eyes," I said to Mrs. Bagoong. "What would it—"

A plump figure barged in front of me. "I say, dear madam," he said. "Could a poor bloke please have another of those heavenly muffins?"

Mrs. Bagoong's smile sent dimples burrowing into her scaly face. "Why, how you talk," said the big iguana. "There's one left, just for you."

She lifted the golden muffin with her tongs.

"But!" I squawked. "That's mine!"

The queen of the lunchroom raised an eyebrow. "Now, now. This charming penguin asked first, and he asked politely."

"But—"

Mrs. Bagoong's frown could have brought on an eclipse at high noon. "Why, Chet Gecko," she said. "I'm surprised at you. Can't you be generous with the new boy?"

"New boy?"

I stepped back to size up the muffin thief.

His webbed feet were planted wide, to support his swollen belly. The penguin's broad butt tapered

to a small head, giving him the look of a bowling pin that needed to hit Weight Watchers.

Topping it all off were a midnight blue bow tie and bowler that would've looked better on a banker than a school kid.

Having snagged my treat, the creature turned with a vague smile.

"Don't believe we've met," he said, extending a flipper. "The name's Bland. James Bland."

He reeked of fermented fish and onions.

My eyes watered. I returned the briefest handshake. "Gecko. Chet Gecko."

Mrs. Bagoong beamed. "So nice to see y'all getting along. James, you've found a new friend already."

"Friend?" I said. "Now, wait just—"

The lunch lady's glare cut me off like a sushi chef hacking a halibut. "Chet will be *happy* to show you around, introduce you." Her eyes completed the thought: *If he ever wants to have seconds in my lunchroom again.*

I heaved a sigh. A good detective can tell when he's outmaneuvered.

"All right, Bland. Come on."

"Good-o," said the penguin. "Ta-ta, madam!" He waved a flipper at Mrs. Bagoong, who simpered back at him. And if you don't think the sight of a simpering iguana is enough to curdle your French fries, think again.

4

I shuffled toward the nearest table. "So, uh, where are you from?"

"Down Under actually, but I've spent donkey's years in Albion," he said.

"Living with a donkey?"

"No, living in England."

Swell. Not only was he a muffin bandit, the guy could barely speak English.

I eyeballed his plate. "Pretty big dessert after such a full meal. Need help?"

"Oh, I'll muddle through," said James Bland. He plunged his beak into the treat and gobbled down about half of it.

So much for the old guilt trick.

A ragtag group of kids ringed the table. Among them sat Frenchy LaTrine, Bo and Tony Newt, Cassandra the Stool Pigeon, and Shirley Chameleon (who had a wicked crush on me)—all eating, laughing, and spraying food.

"Hey, sports fans," I said. "This is James Blond."

"Bland," said the penguin.

"Ain't that the truth," I said. "Anyway, he's a new kid, from Down Over."

"Under," said Bland.

"Whatever." I gestured to the group. "James, guys; guys, James."

The penguin bowed. "A pleasure to make your acquaintance," he said.

Frenchy LaTrine giggled. "Cool accent!"

"Do you know any kangaroos personally?" asked Tony Newt.

"A few," said the penguin. He scarfed down the rest of the muffin as I watched sadly. "I say, do you know what they call a lazy kangaroo?"

"No, what?" said Frenchy.

"A pouch potato," said Bland.

The girls shrieked with laughter; even my buddy Bo chuckled.

I didn't care. So what if the new guy was funny?

Shirley Chameleon elbowed Bo Newt. "Scoot over for James."

She didn't suggest they make room for me.

The penguin squeezed his bubble butt in between them. He vacuumed the last muffin fragments off Shirley's plate.

"What do you do for *fun,* James?" she asked, batting her eyes.

I didn't care. Although Shirley had a crush on *me,* she was free to fling her cooties wherever she wanted.

Bland angled his hat. "Actually, I do a spot of detective work," he said.

Now, wait just a boll-weevil-pickin' minute.

"Fascinating!" said Frenchy, resting her paw on his flipper. "Tell us more!"

The penguin leaned forward. "Well, on one occasion, Her Majesty rang me up for a special—"

My face went all hot.

"*You* know the Queen of England?" I said.

"Rather."

"Sure, and I know the pope."

"Really?" said Bland, half turning. "Does he mention me often?"

I spluttered.

The kids shushed me. "Ignore the lizard," said Frenchy. "Go on, James."

"So when the crown jewels went missing— I say, you're not saving that last bit of eggplant, are you?"

Wordlessly, the mouse slid her tray over.

My tail curled.

"Thanks awfully," said Bland. He slurped up her leftovers. "Now, where was I . . . ?"

"The crown jewels," said Shirley. She shouted over to the next table, "Hey, you guys! He was a detective for the queen!"

"You don't actually believe this bozo?" I choked. "He's making it up!"

Shirley twisted to look at me. "Oh, Chet," she said. "You, of all people."

"Yeah," said Frenchy. "Listen and learn!"

"Learn?!"

The table of kids ignored me. They were riveted

by Bland's bogus tale of jewel thieves, secret passages, and narrow escapes.

Someone tugged on my arm. "Chet?"

It was my partner, a wisecracking mockingbird named Natalie Attired. She nodded toward the door. I followed.

"I don't get it," I said.

"Why, despite years of daylight saving time, we've still only got twenty-four hours in a day?"

"No," I said. "Why they fall for that . . . that potbellied fraud."

"What's wrong with the penguin?" asked Natalie.

I ticked off his faults. "He stuffs his face constantly, all the girls flirt with him, he tells bad jokes, and on top of that, he claims to be a detective."

Natalie eyed me. "*Hmm,* sounds a lot like someone I know."

"I'm serious."

"Ah, the green-eyed monster has raised its ugly head."

"Herman?"

"No, bug breath. Jealousy." She rested a wing tip on my shoulder. "You're jealous of him."

"Of James *Bland*? No way."

"Yup," said Natalie. "And I know just how to get you over it."

"How? Drop him into a vat of boiling broccoli?"

She shook her head. "Start a new case."

Despite my grumpiness, the corners of my lips tugged upward. "All right, then. But this penguin PI better keep his beak out of it."

"Don't worry," said Natalie.

But I did, a little. And before long, I'd wish that I'd worried a whole lot more.

2

When Bush Comes to Shove

Natalie and I hoofed it past clumps of kids on the playground. They were chasing soccer balls, shooting hoops, running and screaming—in short, acting like this was their last lunch break on earth.

That's Emerson Hicky Elementary. Live fast, play hard, and hope the teachers don't call on you.

We were headed for our unofficial office—the cool shade of the scrofulous tree—where a client waited.

"She was a little vague," said Natalie. "But she really needs our help."

"That's me, Helpful Harry," I said.

"Just so long as you're not Cranky Chettie. She's kinda shy."

When we reached the scrofulous tree, the place was deserted.

"Sure you got the right time?" I asked.

"Sure, I'm sure," said Natalie.

I scanned our surroundings again. "Then where's our client?"

"Right here," said a voice as dry as a camel's earwax.

"Right where?" I asked.

Squinting, I made her out: a little sparrow the same color as the scrofulous tree. "Sister, that's some protective coloration," I said.

She was a symphony in brown—brown feathers, brown purse, and a brown wool cap that looked like it had come out on the losing end of a fight with killer moths. She was the kind of kid you could sit beside every day and never notice.

"I'm uh, Ginger Vitus," she said.

"How nice for you," I said.

"Natalie says you're detectives."

"We've been called that."

Natalie and I sat; Ginger stood and stared down at her claws.

"So . . . what's the job?" I asked when she didn't speak. "Deranged boyfriend? Stolen documents? Killer robots?"

The sparrow fiddled with her purse. "Um, not exactly. It's my sister—"

"She's been kidnapped and you want us to find her!" said Natalie.

"No, she's, uh, fallen in with the wrong crowd—"

"And you want us to infiltrate the gang!" I said.

Ginger blinked. "Are you two always this, um, obnoxious?"

"Sorry," I said. "It's an off day."

"Usually, we're worse," said Natalie.

The sparrow cocked her head. "I'd like you to keep an eye on my sister Conjuncti, uh, Connie. I'm afraid something might happen to her."

"Like what?" I said.

"Something awful," said Ginger.

Natalie smirked. "Well, that narrows it down."

"Have you tried talking to your sister?" I asked.

Ginger twisted her purse strap. Moisture gathered in her big brown eyes, like a science project on condensation. (So sue me; I got a good grade on that project.)

"She won't listen to me anymore," said Ginger. Her beak quivered.

I held up a palm. "Spare us the waterworks. Let's get this straight: Basically, you want us to keep an eye on Connie and make sure nothing bad happens?"

"That's right."

"That's all?" asked Natalie.

"Um, yes."

I shook my head.

"What?" asked Ginger.

"You don't want a private eye. You want a baby-sitter." I stood up. "Natalie, let's buzz this beehive."

"But Chet . . . ," said Natalie.

I turned toward the blacktop.

Chinga-ching ching! A coin purse jingled.

"I'll pay you," said Ginger. "Plenty."

I turned back. "Sister, that should've been the first thing you said. Now, where can we find sweet little Connie, and what does she look like?"

Two minutes later, Natalie and I were leaning on a pole, watching a young sparrow in a pink crop top do the swing thing.

"Yup, that's her," said Natalie, comparing the real Connie to the photo Ginger had given us.

"Looks just like her sister," I said.

"Yup."

We watched the girl swing for another minute.

"Okay, I'm bored," I said.

"Me, too," said Natalie.

I scanned the area. "See any shady characters?"

"Besides you?" said Natalie. "Nope."

We were quiet for another minute. Connie kept on swinging.

"Okay, now I'm *really* bored," I said.

"Me, three," said Natalie.

Digging in my pocket, I fished out some coins. "No reason both of us should die of dullness. Why don't I use some of our client's money to buy sodas?"

"Why don't *I* do it?" said Natalie. "After all, you're the one in the detective outfit."

I shrugged. "Fine. Suit yourself."

Natalie flew off for refreshments. I kept my eyeballs peeled.

This wasn't our most exciting case ever. It wasn't even the second most exciting. In fact, it was about as thrilling as watching a garden slug marathon in Big Lump, Montana.

The sparrow swung back and forth... back and forth... back and forth...

The autumn sunshine warmed my bones with its gentle glow. I yawned.

My eyes couldn't have been closed for more than a couple seconds. But the next thing I knew, Connie was hustling off with a skunk, a seagull, and two rough-looking badgers.

"*Hey!*" I pushed away from the pole and rushed after them.

The gull slipped into the bushes, Connie right behind him. The other three shoved a thick branch aside and followed.

I plunged into the greenery on their heels. "Connie, wait up—"

Whunk!

The branch whapped me in the face like a power hitter's home-run swing.

I did what any tough private eye would do.

I collapsed like a ton of bricks.

My memory of the next little bit was clouded by a King Kong–sized headache and the fact that everything was spinning like a kindergartner learning to cartwheel. But I can say this for sure: Two worried faces were leaning over me.

"Are you all right, Chet?" asked Natalie.

"*All right?*" shrilled Ginger Vitus. "I give him one simple task: protect my sister. Now *she's* kidnapped, while *he's* taking a nap. How is that all right?"

15

"Eh, uh..." The answer was right on the tip of my tongue.

But then it, and the rest of me, vanished down a long, long tunnel that opened into blackness.

3

Dr. Heckle and Sister Hide

I awoke on a hard pallet that smelled of disinfectant, tears, and lollipops. My forehead felt colder than a tattletale's heart.

Nurse Marge Supial poked me in the leg. "Does that hurt?" she asked.

"Not much," I groaned.

The sturdy wombat prodded my stomach. "And this?"

"Hee, hee—no!"

She lifted the ice pack and felt my head. "How about this?"

"*Oooh*. Only when I blink."

Nurse Supial shook her gray-furred noggin. "Lad, your talents are wasted here."

"Really?"

"You should be on the stage." She shook a couple of aspirin from a bottle and handed them to me with a cup of water. "Take these."

I swallowed the pills. "What, no lollipop?"

Nurse Supial crossed her arms. "They're for sickies, not *sickos*. Off with you."

So much for the healing touch.

I shuffled back to class. The pain faded, but it seemed my headache was just beginning. Word of my foul-up had spread like melted yak butter on toast.

There's no news like bad news.

And I got another dose of it when I scuffed into my classroom. That pesky penguin, James Bland, was sitting at a desk up front.

The new kid was in my class.

I eased into my seat.

The prissy gopher in the next row looked around. "I heard you blew a case today," said Bitty Chu. "Got knocked out by a little old bush."

She giggled, and Olive Drabb the field mouse joined her.

"Watch out for Mr. Ratnose's fern," she droned. "It's got a mean left hook."

They chortled together.

"Settle down!" said Mr. Ratnose. "This is quiet reading time, not a sewing circle."

I propped a copy of *A Wrinkle in Slime* on my desk and pretended to read, but questions whirled around in my brain like a weasel in a washing machine.

How could I have been so careless on the playground? Where had Connie gone? And what was the capital of Mississippi? (We had to memorize ten state capitals for tomorrow's quiz.)

I fingered the lump on my forehead. It throbbed. My teeth clenched.

Those punks couldn't bop me and get away with it. No badger makes a monkey out of Chet Gecko.

I hopped to my feet, ready to roll. Nothing could stop me.

"Chet Gecko, where do you think you're going?"

Except my teacher.

"Um, I . . . still feel woozy," I said, swaying.

The lean rat squinted at me. "Ten-minute bathroom break."

"Thanks, Mr. Ratnose." For maximum sympathy, I weaved toward the door. My acting would fool anyone.

"One more thing," said Mr. Ratnose.

"Hmm?"

"Come right back, Chester Gecko."

I hate it when they call me by my full name.

As soon as I was out of sight, I hightailed it down the hall, making for the scene of Connie's abduction.

With luck, maybe I could pick up some clues before the trail grew cold.

The playground was as still as a vampire condo at high noon. I trotted straight to the bushes where I'd last seen Connie.

Thanks to a recent watering, the mud held footprints. I recognized badger, skunk, gull, and sparrow tracks, as well as the imprint of a big gecko booty.

Hmm . . . I must have really landed hard.

On the far side of the shrubbery, the gull and paw prints continued, but the sparrow tracks disappeared. Odd.

Bent low, I scanned the ground in widening circles, but picked up no further sign. Ginger's sister hadn't just sprouted wings and flown away. Had she?

Oh, wait. She was a sparrow.

So maybe she *had* flown, or been carried off. But where to?

I straightened and surveyed the school yard again. Nothing. No use trying to find the kidnappers now; they were either off studying or playing hooky.

What to do, what to do?

Fresh out of ideas, I returned to class. They like it when you do that once in a while.

Late recess found me raring to go. In the logjam at the door, I heard the penguin call, "I say, Chet old bean!"

20

I turned. "Yeah, old . . . carrot?"

James Bland straightened his bowler. "In just a bit, I'm going to treat some of the lads to a cricket match," he said. "Care to join us?"

"You're lighting crickets?"

"No, actually," said Bland. "Playing it."

I frowned. "I don't play crickets; I eat them."

"Oh," he said. "Perhaps some other time."

When warthogs learn to play kazoo, I thought. But I only said, "I'm on a case."

"Do let me know if you need my help, won't you?"

Grandma Gecko would've been proud. I didn't say any of the thirteen nasty things that came to mind. I just nodded stiffly and skedaddled.

Fast though I was, Natalie already waited beneath the scrofulous tree. "Ready for a rematch with that shrub?" she said. "Or are you feeling bushed?"

"Ha and ha," I said. "I'd rather go grill our client, Ginger Vitus."

She stretched a wing. "Not sure she'll like that. Last time I saw Ginger, she was bad-mouthing you all over school."

I squared my shoulders. "I don't care if she's taking out TV ads calling me a bug-eating boob. Her sister vanished on my watch, and nobody knows more about Connie than Ginger. She's *got* to talk to us."

"If you say so, slugger," said Natalie.

21

We waded into the swirl of kids that washed over the school yard like a snot-nosed tide. At last, we found Ginger in a small herd of nerds, chattering away.

(How did I know they were nerds? I'm a trained detective. Plus, there were enough calculators, pocket protectors, and clunky glasses among them to supply a small geek convention.)

They were the chemistry club. And they looked it.

The group fell silent as we approached. Someone whispered loudly, "Isn't that the lame-o gecko who lost Connie?"

I winced. My reputation may not be worth much, but it's all that I've got.

"Ginger," I said, "can we talk to you alone?"

The sparrow peered past one of the ugliest bunnies I've ever seen. "Why should I?" huffed Ginger. "Have you found some new way to, uh, ruin my life?"

"We'd like to know more about Connie," said Natalie.

"She's missing, and you're responsible," said the sparrow. "What more is there to know?"

Her beak quivered, and Frankenbunny patted Ginger's shoulder.

"Basic stuff," I said. "Her friends, her usual haunts, the names of the punks she went off with."

"Why in the, uh, world would you want that?"

I put my hands on my hips. "Because in case you didn't notice, Miss Smartie-Beak, we're trying to find your sister."

"Don't. You've done enough damage already."

"Think nothing of it," said Natalie. "That's our job."

"Not anymore," said the sparrow. "You're both fired."

My mouth fell open. "What?"

"But how will you find your sister?" asked Natalie.

A half smile played across Ginger's face. "I've found a *real* detective."

"What do you mean?" I asked.

A familiar chubby bird stepped out from behind the nerds. "No worries, chap," said the penguin. "James Bland is on the case!"

4

Raging Gull

My gut clenched, worse than that time I won the scorpion burrito-eating contest. Words staggered from my mouth like a centipede trying to cha-cha.

"You . . . uh, he? How . . . er? I mean . . ."

"Pip-pip," said the penguin. "I'll have this all sorted out by teatime, won't I?"

"You will?" I said.

Ginger favored Bland with a grateful smile. "Thanks, James. You're the best." She glared at me. "I should know; I've tried the rest."

"Hey," I said. "It wasn't my fault."

The sparrow turned her back on me, and her friends followed suit.

"Were any of you there when Connie was

snatched?" asked Natalie. "Can you help us? Any-one?"

Nobody looked our way. Nobody spoke.

"No problem," I said. "We'll solve it without you, or I'm not the finest detective at Emerson Hicky."

"That's right," someone muttered. "You're not."

I stiffened.

Natalie grabbed my arm. "Easy, big gecko." She steered me away across the grass. For a while, neither of us spoke.

"That," I said at last, "was about as useful as lacy bloomers on a raging bull."

"But not nearly as colorful," she said. "So, what've we got, Mr. Private Eye?"

I looked across the playground. "Well, we've got no clues."

"No client," said Natalie.

"No class," I said.

"Then what's left?"

Jingling the coins in my pocket, I said, "Fifty cents and our good looks."

"Think that's enough?" said Natalie.

"It's enough for a snack," I said. "And that's a start."

Fortified by half a Pillbug Crunch bar, Natalie and I decided to kick the case into high gear. We would find Connie's kidnappers or know the reason why.

At the scene of the crime, we spotted two third graders playing Frisbee. One was a rat whose wavy fur looked like she'd had a bad perm job. The other was a dim-looking mole wearing a hand-lettered T-shirt that read, PROUD TO BE RILLY COOL.

"Hey, señorita," I said to Wavy Rat. "Were you here at lunchtime?"

"What if I was?" she said.

"Did you see those tough guys take Connie Vitus?" asked Natalie.

The rat glanced at her pal. "What if we did?"

"Can you tell us anything?" I asked. "Their names? Where they hang out? Where they went?"

"Ur, what's in it for us?" asked Cool Mole.

"Why do you two always answer a question with a question?" asked Natalie.

"What do you mean?" said Wavy Rat.

I sized them up. They were pretty wise for third graders, but they were still third graders.

"What's in it for you?" I said. "The satisfaction of helping Justice triumph, and rescuing an innocent girl from the road to ruin."

The pair looked at me, then at each other.

"What else do we get?" said Cool Mole.

Tch. Kids today.

"What's the big deal?" I said. "Just say what you know. It's not like we're asking you to rat on anybody."

Wavy Rat narrowed her eyes.

"No offense," I said.

"None taken," she said. "But I have a bad memory."

I reached into my pocket. "Would half a Pillbug Crunch bar help it?"

The chocolate vanished from my grip in the blink of a mosquito's eyelash.

"Now you're talkin'," said the mole. "Ur, what did you want again?"

The rat broke the candy bar in two and handed half to her buddy. "They wanted to know about Charles de Gull and his gang."

"Is that the seagull's name?" asked Natalie.

"Yeah," said Cool Mole. "But I wouldn't mess with him if I was you."

"Why not?" I asked.

"Ur, you know the bike rack bullies?"

I nodded. Everyone knew the punks who hung out by the bike racks.

"These guys are even worse," said Wavy Rat.

Natalie's eyes grew big. "Connie was last seen with them. Now she's gone."

The rat glanced behind me. "Uh-oh," she said. "Time for *us* to get gone."

I swiveled.

Speak of the devil. Charles de Gull, the skunk, and the badgers stood by the swings, big as life and twice as surly. The badgers held two first graders suspended, while the gull demanded something.

I turned to thank our informants, but all I saw were their tails, hightailing it away from the scene.

Detectives are made of sterner stuff.

"Ready?" I asked Natalie.

She spread a wing. "After you, tough guy."

When we reached the swing set, Charles de Gull was counting a fistful of change, and the first graders had run off, sniffling. At our approach, the badgers flexed and growled.

"You Charles de Gull?" I asked the bird.

"Phht," the seagull scoffed. His sneer was strong enough to curdle mantis milk. A black eye patch hid one eye. "You 'ave come to geev us ze money?"

"No, we have come to ask the questions."

"Woh, ho, ho!" he laughed. "Ze saucy gecko eez looking for trouble."

The skunk burped. "He's come to the right place," she said. "We got trouble up the wazoo."

"I don't care about your digestive problems," I said. "Tell me about Connie Vitus."

De Gull pouted thoughtfully. "Zees name, she rings no bells with me. Zibo?"

"Don't know any Connies," said the skunk, frowning. "But I got Kristas and Brittneys for days."

"Cute as a bucket full of kittens," I said. "I'd almost believe you if I hadn't seen you with the girl at lunchtime."

"Where's Connie?" asked Natalie. "Did you kidnap her?"

The teasing tone disappeared from the seagull's voice. It was all steel and gravel now. "Zees eez a very serious charge," he said, waddling toward us with menace. "And I am getting sick and tired of answering eet."

The twin badgers stepped forward. Natalie and I backed up.

"What do you mean, *tired*?" said my partner. "Who else accused you?"

The seagull spat. "Zat foolish penguin who thinks he eez a private eye."

Well, at least de Gull and I agreed on one thing.

"And what did you tell him?" I asked.

"What I tell you," said the bird. "Zat I never heard of zees Connie. Eef you keep sticking your nose in my beeswax, I will knock your biscuit all the way to Bogotá."

Charles de Gull snapped his wing tip (no mean trick) and the badgers moved.

I didn't wait around to witness their biscuit-knocking skills. Natalie and I beat feet, with the goons hot on our heels. We scrambled across the blacktop and blundered into a game.

Thonk!

Getting nailed by a dodgeball probably didn't help the lead badger's mood. The big oaf stopped to threaten the ball thrower.

Natalie and I blasted through a basketball practice and didn't stop until we reached the shelter of the nearest classroom. Our pursuers had given up.

"Well, that was ... something," said Natalie.

I panted, hands on knees. "Something I ... don't care to repeat. What do you ... think?"

Natalie cocked her head. "They got awfully steamed by some simple questions."

"Maybe it's just a ... smoke screen," I said.

"Maybe," said Natalie. "And where there's smoke ..."

"There's coughing."

"So why don't we—"

But before we could hatch a plan, the class bell rang.

I groused. "Real detectives don't have these interruptions."

"Not true," she said. "Even Sherlock Holmes had to answer to a school bell."

"Yeah?" I asked. "What kind of school bell?"

"Elementary, my dear Chetson."

5

TV or Not TV

Afternoon lessons limped by. Science class was a snooze. Why we can't study something useful, like robot design or alien autopsies, I'll never know.

Maybe it was my imagination, but when I botched a geology question, more than the usual scorn and laughter showered me. And when James Bland shared an iceberg tale from his Antarctica field trip, the class applauded.

The penguin half bowed from his seat.

I chewed my lip.

After a couple more rounds of boredom and humiliation, our teacher turned on Emerson Hicky's student news program. I welcomed the distraction.

Vice Principal Shrewer's sour puss filled the TV

screen. "Listen up, students," she snapped. "It's Wednesday, and time for the news. So shut your yap."

The camera lingered on her face for long seconds, while Ms. Shrewer held the pained grimace that passed for her smile. Finally, she hissed at the camera operator, "On the anchor, you lamebrain!"

The image jerked and swung wildly, ending up on a bird's clawed feet. "I'm Elise— On my *face,* you dweeb!" said a girl's voice.

Ah, the glamour of live television.

Finally the camera tilted up to reveal a robin sporting a cheery grin. "I'm Elise Navidad, and this is *Emerson Hicky Today,*" chirped the bird. "In our news: A child goes missing, and fourth-grade detective Chet Gecko is to blame."

Oh, great. My day was complete.

Elise ran down the basic details with an evil perkiness. For visuals, they used my rejected school photo—the one where I'd crossed my eyes.

I sank lower in my seat. My classmates stared and hooted.

After what felt like an ice age, the jolly robin wrapped up her report. "But the administration isn't worried. The school's newest detective, James Bland, is hot on the case, and expects to find the missing sparrow by tomorrow."

James Bland's clueless mug appeared on-screen. The real James tipped his bowler to the TV.

"So classy," sighed Bitty Chu.

"So handsome," murmured Shirley Chameleon.

So sick. My lunch threatened to make a reappearance.

The class buzzed. Bland smirked and nodded to the room.

On TV, Elise's sprightly grin threatened to unhinge her eyelashes and send them fluttering off like butterflies. "And here with sports is Neil Down."

The camera switched to Neil, who blathered on about the usual sports stuff. Our crosstown rivalry with Petsadena Elementary, *blah blah blah* . . . the big soccer game on Friday, *yada yada yada* . . .

The report washed over me like lukewarm bathwater. All I could think was: Gotta beat that penguin to the punch.

The rest of the school day passed in a haze (the way it usually did). But when the final bell clanged, I was ready.

I brushed past the pitying glances of my classmates and out into the halls, scouting for Natalie in the after-school crowd. Like kids everywhere, the other students were sympathetic and tactful.

"Hey, Gecko," squawked a parrot. "Way to blow a case!"

A squirrel giggled. "I've got a brother I'd like to lose. Wanna watch him?"

I gritted my teeth and plowed onward. Just outside her classroom, Natalie was coaxing a couple of extra-credit homework questions from her teacher, Amanda Reckonwith.

Some dames can't get enough torture.

I pulled her aside. "Think you could forget about schoolwork for a minute and focus on the important stuff?"

"Like what?" she asked.

"Our reputation."

Natalie smirked. "You mean *your* reputation. They didn't mention me."

I rolled my eyes. "You gonna help or not?"

"Don't get your tail in a twist," she said. "I'm coming."

Methodically, we cast our dragnet, looking for any sign of Connie, or failing that, of the Gull gang.

We searched behind the portables. Nothing.

We scoped out the rooftops. Nada.

We poked around the cafeteria. Not even a stray butterscotch cricket cookie.

"We'll never find her," I said.

"Can't you be more positive?" asked Natalie.

"Okay. I'm positive we'll never find her."

On our way out to the playground, Natalie asked, "Did anything about our last meeting with Ginger seem weird to you?"

"Like what?"

"Think about it. She hires us to protect her sister, and then when Connie *really* needs our help, she *fires* us."

"*Hmm.* When you put it that way, it does seem a little wacko."

With a stroke of good luck, we bumped into Connie's teacher, Claire Voyant, doing bus duty at the playground's edge. With a stroke of bad luck, she had no helpful information.

The mud hen fluffed her feathers. "I think it's best you don't get involved. Let the pro handle it. Have you heard that James Bland found the Lost City of Atlantis? Or was it the Abominable Snowman?"

"I'll show *him* abomina—" I began.

Natalie towed me off. "Thanks a bunch!" she told the teacher.

"I'd like to clean that penguin's cuckoo clock," I said as we crossed the grass.

"If you really want to show him up, you know what you do?"

"What?"

"Find the girl," said Natalie.

I couldn't argue with that. Halfheartedly, I scanned the playground again. Then Natalie clutched my arm.

"Over there," she said. "De Gull and his gang."

Before they could spot us, we hustled behind the slides. Natalie and I peeked out around the edges.

"Perfect-o," I said. "We follow them; they lead us to Connie."

Charles de Gull and his buddies terrorized a straggling third grader. After the little wren flew off, the gang split up. Charles and Zibo headed toward the gym, while the badgers trundled over to the last bus.

"Shall we?" said Natalie.

"After you, birdie."

We gave seagull and skunk a head start. Then Natalie and I trailed behind, dodging from bush to pole to trash can. That's the PI way.

The punks suspected nothing. They never once looked back.

"How could they have stashed Connie in the gym?" I said. "We went over it with a fine-tooth comb."

"Maybe we should've used a brush, too," said Natalie.

Charles and Zibo pushed through the wide gymnasium doors.

We lurked outside for a ten-count, then pussy-footed after (or in my case, gecko-footed).

Late afternoon rays slanted through the skylights. The gym was emptier than a promise from a hungry shark.

I pointed toward the locker rooms. Natalie took the GIRLS; I took the BOYS. No point in risking cooties by mixing it up.

Someone was banging around inside. Had de Gull squirreled Connie away in a locker? (Could you squirrel a sparrow?) I crept forward and peeked around the corner, down low.

It was the seagull, all right—slipping into a golden soccer jersey.

Clever disguise. But it couldn't fool Chet Gecko.

Charles slammed his locker and boogied out the back door. I eased over and checked it out. Nothing but Ace bandages and stinky sweatsocks.

Cautiously, I poked my head out the back door. Charles de Gull flapped his way toward the field, followed closely by a jogging Zibo, also in a jersey.

Hmm.

Natalie slipped around the corner of the building. We tailed the pair. Bleachers and high bushes blocked our view of the field.

A whistle blast knifed through the air.

"Is de Gull signaling the rest of his gang?" said Natalie.

"One way to find out," I said.

We hustled over to the bushes and flopped onto our bellies. (Maybe we didn't need to, but that's how they do it in spy movies.) Together, we wormed along to a gap in the greenery and peered through.

What we saw made my jaw drop.

"They're playing soccer," said Natalie.

"Now what," I said, "is up with that?"

6

On a Wing and a Player

Although Natalie and I watched for half an hour, Charles de Gull and Zibo did nothing suspicious at soccer practice. (Unless you count kicking the ball out of bounds, but half the team did that.)

Mostly they warmed the bench and sulked.

Coach Beef Stroganoff bawled encouragement at the players. "How you gonna beat Petsadena? My mother plays better than you!"

(Of course, he didn't mention that his mother, a former pro wrestler and rugby star, could also bench-press a Buick.)

"I don't get it," I said. "What does soccer have to do with a missing girl?"

"Beats me," said Natalie. "But here's another question for you."

"Shoot."

"What tea do soccer players drink?"

"Huh?"

"PenalTea!" She cackled.

I groaned. Obviously we'd learned nothing useful watching the practice. And I didn't know how many more of Natalie's jokes I could take.

We retrieved my skateboard and rolled on home.

The next morning dawned as cloudy as my brain. I couldn't make heads or tails of this case. Nobody had any leads on the missing girl, and the supposed kidnappers would rather play soccer than send ransom notes.

Recess that day brought its fair share of surprises. And I don't mean the finding-a-Three-Mosquitoes-bar-in-your-book-bag kind, or the teacher-forgot-all-about-the-homework-which-you-didn't-do-any-way variety.

The fun began while I punched a tetherball, brooding on the case. Bitty Chu trotted up with a smug expression. (Not an unusual look for a teacher's pet.)

"Chet, did you hear the news?" she asked.

"What, you finally saved up enough for that lobotomy?" I said.

Bitty planted her paws on her furry hips. "Guess again, wisenheimer. Someone else found Ginger Vitus's sister."

"Connie's been found?" I stopped dead. The ball swung around the pole and bopped me in the gut. "By—*unh!*—who?"

"By *whom*," said Bitty, a lifelong member of the Grammar Police. "It's James Bland! Not only is he cuter, he's a way better detective than you are."

"That yo-yo? He couldn't find his left nostril with a flipper jammed in it up to the third knuckle."

Bitty batted her eyes. "Ooh, jealous?" she said.

"That'll be the day." I turned and swaggered off toward the scrofulous tree.

Never let 'em see you sweat.

"I guess it's true what they say," the gopher called after me. "You've lost your touch."

"Maybe, but I've found your smell," I said, fanning a hand before my face.

Once away from Bitty, I dropped the pose. *Found your smell?* What a weak comeback. My touch wasn't all I was losing.

I deflated faster than a blimp that bumped the Eiffel Tower. How could a doofus with the IQ of a soggy cucumber find the missing girl when I couldn't?

It wasn't fair.

As I dragged my sorry tail over to the tree, Natalie glided down to land.

"Hey there, frowny face," she said. "Hang on, I've got just the cure."

"Not now," I said.

But my mockingbird pal was unstoppable.

"Knock, knock," she said.

I stared, mute.

"Who's there?" Natalie answered in my voice.

"Euripides."

"Euripides who?" said Natalie-as-me.

"Euripides pants, I breaka you face!" She spread her wings and grinned.

When I didn't react, Natalie leaned closer. "Hey, you really *are* blue. What's got you down, partner?"

I sank onto a tree root and spilled the beans.

"That can't be right," said Natalie.

"It's not," I said. "But it's what I heard."

"But you can't—I can't—we can't just take this," said Natalie. She hopped to and fro, clawing the dirt. "We've gotta get up, get out there, and...and..."

"He found her," I said. "I didn't. Case closed."

Natalie gazed at me a moment. Then she rested a wing tip on my shoulder.

"Chet, I still think you're the best detective ever."

"Really?"

"No, I think you're a bug-eating moron," she said. "Of course, *really*. Something's odd here, and we're going to get to the bottom of it."

"But—"

Natalie pulled me to my feet. "But me no buts," she said. "You're a private eyeball. Let's do some private eyeballing."

She bumped me with her head to get me moving.

"Hey, I thought you said no butts," I said.

It wasn't hard to find James Bland. We just looked for his penguin posse. He stood near the cafeteria, ringed by a mob, smiling and making modest faces.

Beside him were Ginger Vitus and a smaller sparrow, probably her sister.

The school's TV camera captured their every move.

"Can never thank him, uh, enough," Ginger was droning into a microphone. "James is the best detective at this—"

Elise Navidad whisked her mike away before the sparrow had half finished. "Great, whatever," she burbled. "And now let's hear from the bird of the hour, the dashing James Bland."

A dark expression flashed across Ginger's face. Nobody likes to lose the spotlight.

The tubby penguin held up a flipper. "All in a day's work," said Bland. "I just sussed out the situation, grasped the nettle, and had done with it, didn't I?"

"Er, did you?" asked Elise.

"Was it dangerous?" cooed Frenchy LaTrine.

"No more than when I single-handedly trounced an evil genius and his army of laser-eyed barracuda. I stowed away aboard a submarine, you see, and—"

The reporter frowned. "Connie was in the submarine?"

"Er, no," said Bland. "You've got your stories muddled, old girl."

At the edge of the crowd, I turned to Natalie. "She's not the only one. He stole that barracuda bit from a James Bond movie."

"Shh!" she said. "I'm trying to listen."

Elise leaned closer to Bland. "So, Jamesy, who kidnapped Connie?"

"Oh, the usual bad lot," said the penguin, adjusting his bowler. "But after a bit of argy-bargy, they packed it in. And I brought the bird home, I did."

The reporter furrowed her brow. The crowd applauded.

Bland gave Connie a squeeze, and she forced a smile.

"Poor thing," I said. "She must still be in shock."

"Mmm," said Natalie, thoughtfully.

As the cheers died down, I shouted, "What clues led you to Connie?"

"Eh?" said Bland. He looked about. "Oh, uh, the usual bits and bobs. Paw prints, secret codes, the dog that didn't bark—that sort of thing."

My teeth gritted. "Can you be any more vague? Exactly *how* did you solve it?"

At last, the penguin spotted me. And so did the TV camera.

"*How* I found the poor girl is not important," said Bland. "What jolly well matters is that I jolly well *found* her, eh?" He appealed to the crowd.

"That's right!" a buff bobcat growled.

Elise Navidad gripped her mike. "Rival detective Chet Gecko is challenging the plucky penguin. Has he gone green with jealousy?"

The rabble rumbled.

"I'm *already* green," I said. "I was born that way."

"Leave James alone!" shouted a feisty porcupine. "He's a hero!"

"Yeah!" chorused the mob.

I held up a hand. "I'm just asking how this fish-slurping bozo did it. Something's screwy here."

"Yeah, your attitude," snarled an iguana the size of a washer-dryer.

Natalie tapped my shoulder. "Uh, Chet? This might be a good time to—"

"And the crowd is getting ugly," trilled Elise Navidad. "They're going to show this has-been PI a thing or two."

She was right. In a blink, the group's mood had switched from celebration to outrage. It wanted blood—my blood.

And I wasn't in the mood to donate.

"Natalie, let's—"

Wings beat behind me, and claws snagged my collar.

"Hang on!" cried Natalie.

She flapped like mad and we rose. Paws snatched at my tail and feet.

Too slow.

We needed a miracle.

Rrrrring!

The class bell cut through the clamor like a hot knife through mealworm pie. What a sweet sound. Kids blinked and looked around, giving up the chase.

But the beefy iguana wasn't finished. He seized my tail and yanked hard.

Ka-*toom*!

Natalie and I tumbled from the sky, smack into a trash can.

"Ow!" I glared at the big reptile. "What'd you do that for?"

The iguana shrugged. "I hate to leave a job half finished." Then he wiped his hands and joined the other kids heading back to class.

"Just our luck," said Natalie. "A perfectionist."

7

Sparrow Change

All through the long stretch before lunch, I nursed my jangled nerves. How could everyone have turned on me? And how could I have been out-detected by Bland—someone so clueless he thought Meow Mix was a CD for cats?

I had no idea.

At the front of the class, the penguin basked in his fame. Shirley and Cassandra slipped him notes. Mr. Ratnose beamed each time he walked past the chubby doofus. And even Waldo the furball left a Termite Twinkie on his desk.

Lunch didn't improve matters. My stock was sinking faster than a lead doughnut. Even tick taco salad and mosquito burritos couldn't lift my spirits.

After the meal, Natalie stretched. "Ready to investigate?" she said.

"Connie?" I said. "I dunno. Everyone will think it's just sour grapes."

"So, we'll make sour grape juice."

To humor her, I followed my partner to the playground. At the jungle gym, we spotted Connie Vitus climbing with a bunch of other second graders.

"Hey, Connie," said Natalie. "Can we have a word?"

The little sparrow eyed us from her perch on the bars. "Um, I guess so."

"I wanted to report on your kidnapping for our current events unit," said Natalie. "And I was wondering: Where exactly did they hide you?"

"In a nest—uh, a nest of crooks."

Natalie nodded. "And who were these crooks?"

"Didn't James say?"

I jumped in. "We, uh, haven't been able to talk to him yet."

The sparrow spread a wing. "Oh. Well, they were crooks, you know?"

"Uh-huh." Natalie smiled encouragingly.

"What did they look like?" I asked.

Connie shrugged. "Um . . . big? Mean?"

"Was it Charles de Gull and his gang?"

"Well, uh—hey," she said, wide-eyed. "Aren't you that gecko detective?"

"Yup," I said modestly. At least the lower grades still respected me.

"The one everybody's laughing at?"

I cleared my throat. "Uh, yeah."

"Tell us, did Charles kidnap you?" asked Natalie.

The little sparrow frowned. "Um, I don't know if I'm s'posed to say—"

With a flurry of feathers, someone rushed between us and Connie.

"Leave my sister alone!" squawked Ginger Vitus.

"We were just—" said Natalie.

"I know what you were doing!" shrilled the sparrow. "You were making her relive her, uh, nightmare."

She pecked at Natalie and me, driving us back.

"But we didn't mean—" I began.

"I don't care!" said Ginger. "Keep away, or I'm telling Principal Zero."

And with that, she fluttered up to her sister, hissed, "Come, Connie!" and they flew off together.

I scratched my chin. "Touchy birdie, ain't she?"

"I'd say we're off her Valentine's list," said Natalie.

We stood and stared after the dwindling figures of the sparrow sisters.

"Any more bright ideas?" I said.

Natalie frowned. "None that won't get you detention."

And that's how it was, all through lunch period. Nobody would talk to us—not Charles, not Connie, not Ginger. And the only player who could talk—James Bland—was harder to pin down than a roomful of river eels.

In the classroom, he was a no-show. Probably off somewhere doing interviews and signing autographs. It must be nice to be a famous detective.

I blew out a sigh.

Class time passed in the usual way—as if we were strapped to the back of a stupefied snail. By late recess, I could've sworn that I'd aged two years.

Forging onto the playground, I vowed to take one last shot at interrogating Bland. Maybe this time we could shake some straight answers out of the guy.

But deep inside, I was afraid that his answers would make me look more like a loser detective than I already did.

Roaming the school yard, Natalie and I asked after the penguin.

"Haven't seen him," said a teacher on yard duty.

"Oh, you know James? He's the *dreamiest*," said a cheerleader.

"Heard you two had a feud," said Jackdaw Ripper. "Very cool."

But nobody knew where he was. We were about to throw in the towel, when fate intervened, in the shape of the school's most feared fat cat.

Just past the library building, a huge figure loomed from the shadows.

"Hold it right there, Gecko."

It was Mr. Zero, the titanic tomcat who ruled Emerson Hicky with a fist of iron. The kids called him Big Fat Zero. But never to his face—not if they valued their hide.

"Whatever Mr. Ratnose said about the aquarium, it's not true," I said.

Principal Zero smoothed his whiskers. "This isn't about Mr. Ratnose," he purred. "But I'll be sure to check with him later."

Dang. I'd forgotten the first rule of dealing with the principal: Never volunteer information.

"Chet Gecko, it has come to my attention that you have a rivalry with this penguin private eye, James Bland."

"Rivalry?" I said. "Ridiculous."

The big cat's tail twitched. "You called him a fish-slurping bozo."

"Me? Never."

"It's on tape," snapped Mr. Zero.

"Oh, that," I said. I examined my palms for smudges.

"Gecko, I wonder if you'd accompany me to your locker," said the cat.

"Funny," I said, "but I've never wondered that."

He growled, a low rumble like an avalanche on Mount Kilimanjaro.

"Shall we go?" I said.

Our principal led the way. Kids cleared back like you could catch a week of detention just by meeting his eyes.

"Not that I don't cherish these get-togethers, but what's up, boss man?"

Mr. Zero glanced over his shoulder at me. "Eh?"

"Why this sudden interest in my locker?" I said. "Collecting stale sandwiches and forgotten homework?"

His eyebrows drew together. "We'll see."

Natalie elbowed me. I clammed up. Even *I* knew enough not to push it when the big cat was in this kind of mood.

We stopped in front of my locker.

"Open it," said Mr. Zero.

"Okeydokey," I said, twisting the combination lock. "But you're going to be disappointed. Nothing but snips and snails and centipede tails..."

The tumblers clicked, and I opened the locker. "See?"

Natalie gasped. Mr. Zero's ears flattened to his skull.

I turned to look.

Atop my pile of random junk sat James Bland's blue bowler.

"Huh," I said. "How did that get here?"

The principal smiled his someone's-gonna-get-it smile. "That's what the police will want to know."

"The *police*?!" said Natalie.

"Why would they want to talk to me?" I asked.

"Because James Bland has disappeared," said Mr. Zero. "And you're their number-one suspect."

8

Grilling Me Softly

The big tomcat left me to stew in the waiting room while he called the cops.

"But I didn't do anything," I told his secretary, Mrs. Crow.

"That's what they all say, dearie," she rasped.

I leaned forward. "This time I *really* didn't."

"Uh-huh." She sorted through some file folders.

So much for tea and sympathy.

Before long, a pair of blue-uniformed dogs padded into the administration building. They stopped at Mrs. Crow's desk.

"Officers Frick and Frack," said the golden-furred one.

"About the missing kid," said the spotted dog.

Mrs. Crow nodded at the principal's office. "In there, boys."

With a slit-eyed stare, the cops marched past. The odor of canned dog food, damp fur, and intimidation rolled off of them in a funk.

Thirty seconds later, a voice snarled, "Gecko!"

"The principal will see you now," said Mrs. Crow.

I stood and wiped my sweaty palms on my T-shirt.

"Any last words?" said the secretary.

"Don't tell 'em it ended like this," I said. "Tell 'em I said something."

Then I trudged into the crime-and-punishment headquarters of the school: Principal Zero's office.

The scarred black desk squatted dead ahead like a wounded water buffalo. Mr. Zero glowered from behind it. The boys in blue filled his guest chairs.

I stood before the desk and eyed the bowler on top of it. My future at Emerson Hicky was balanced on a knife's edge, and I wasn't much of a gymnast.

"Never," said the principal, "in all my years at this school—never have I had to call the police on a student."

A response didn't seem expected, so I didn't make any.

The cat scowled. "And yet, your behavior leaves me no choice."

Silence was working for me. I did some more of it.

"You'd better tell these officers everything you know about James Bland," said Mr. Zero. "And it better be the truth, because I can sniff out a lie quicker than you can snatch the last cookie off the plate."

My eyes flicked to his colossal gut. The ol' tomcat had been doing a bit of cookie snatching himself. But this didn't seem like the time to mention it.

"Well, Gecko?" said Officer Frick.

I kept on saying nothing. If these two badge bandits were trying to railroad Chet Gecko, they'd get no help from me.

"Cat got your tongue?" said Officer Frack.

No, but he had another part of my anatomy in a sling.

"Speak up," growled the principal.

"Okay," I said at last. "I didn't do it."

"Tell us," said golden-haired Frick.

"Everything," said spotty Frack.

I cleared my throat. "This new kid shows up yesterday, says he's a PI. Ginger Vitus hires him to find her sister. He finds her. Case closed."

"Not quite." Frack twisted the desk lamp so it shone in my face.

I squinted and shaded my eyes. "What's with the light show?"

"You were jealous, weren't you?" said Frick, rising to pace behind me.

"No way," I said.

Principal Zero sniffed twice. "Smells like a fib brewing."

"Okay," I said. "Maybe I was, a little. This smooth-talking mug showed up, grabbed my business, and solved my case."

"You argued," said Frack.

"I argue with lots of people," I said. "Is that a crime?"

"Not yet," said Mr. Zero. "But a principal can always hope."

The golden-haired dog leaned over me. His breath smelled like he'd been drinking his water from someplace other than the fountain, if you get my drift.

"You lost your temper," said Frick. "You kidnapped your rival."

"I didn't!"

"Crime of passion," said Frack. "Oldest story in the book."

"Then get a new book," I said.

Officer Frick turned to Principal Zero. "Is he lying?"

The hefty cat padded over and took a long whiff. He paused. "No," he said. "But my nose isn't a hundred percent accurate."

Frick rested a paw on my shoulder. "Gecko, we got motive, opportunity, and"—he nodded at the bowler—"physical evidence."

"It don't look good," said Frack. His tail wagged.

I glanced from one hard face to another. "Someone planted that hat in my locker. They disappeared Bland, and now they're trying to pin it on me."

"Who would do that?" said Officer Frick.

"I don't know," I said. "Give me till tomorrow to find out."

The principal and the cops exchanged looks. Something passed between them in their secret Authority Figure language.

My tail curled.

"You got until noon tomorrow," said Frack.

"Can we make it three o'clock?" I said. "I've got schoolwork."

Frack held up a paw. "Don't push it."

"Three o'clock," said Frick. "And if you can't prove you were framed, you'll be a guest of our lovely juvenile detention facility."

With urgency in my step, I made for the door. "I'll get right on it."

"Gecko," rumbled Mr. Zero. "Aren't you forgetting something?"

Turning back, I said, "Um, thanks for the chance to clear my name?"

He shook his head and pointed a claw at the wall clock. "Class now, detection later."

I sighed. Tough is the life of a grade-school detective.

9

Eat, Think, and Be Scary

As Mr. Ratnose droned through our lessons, my mind toiled harder than a hamster inside a fifty-foot Ferris wheel. But not on schoolwork.

I mulled over possible suspects, but didn't get very far. I wondered where Bland was, but couldn't puzzle that out, either.

An annoying whine interrupted my thinking. It was my teacher's voice.

"Are you with us, Mr. Gecko?"

"Huh?" I said, looking around.

"I asked you, how do clouds get formed?" said Mr. Ratnose.

I scratched my nose. "Beats me. But the clouds know how to do it, and that's the important thing."

The class laughed, Mr. Ratnose groaned, and I went back to brooding.

After the last bell rang, I hunted up Natalie and told her the latest.

"We've got until three o'clock tomorrow?" she said as we tromped down the hall. "That's not much time."

"You're telling me," I said.

"So what do we know so far?"

I cracked my knuckles. "I know one thing. This job needs our best brainstorming. And that means..."

"Snacks?" said Natalie.

"And plenty of 'em. Let's hit my home office."

Fifteen minutes later, we slipped through the tall grass of the backyard into my own private think tank. The home office sits behind the bamboo, cleverly disguised as a refrigerator box.

Gotta keep those bad guys guessing.

Natalie and I unloaded an armful of potato-bug crisps, gypsy moth brownies, deep-fried dragonfly livers, and sow-bug soda.

That was for me. She had an apple.

Halfway through the snacks, my brain started firing on all cylinders.

"Okay, let's think who could've made James Bland disappear," I said, munching a brownie.

"Well, a celebrity stalker, for starters," said Natalie.

"*Mmm,* or maybe an enemy who followed him from his old school."

She cocked her head. "But why would his old enemy frame you?"

"Good point." I mused while rummaging in the potato-bug crisps. "Aha!"

"You got the suspect?" asked Natalie.

I drew my hand from the bag. "Nope, the prize— a decoder ring."

"Get serious, Chet."

Suddenly, it hit me. "Hey, I know who made the penguin vanish."

"Who?"

"Bland himself."

Natalie rapped on my head. "Hello," she said. "Anybody home? Why would James make himself disappear?"

I upended the bag into my mouth and swallowed the last of the crisps. "Because he wanted to get back at me."

"But *he* found Connie," said Natalie. "He's got the upper hand. *You* should be wanting to get back at *him.*"

"Oh, yeah."

Natalie rose and paced the length of the box. "No, I'm betting it's Connie's kidnappers. The cases are connected somehow."

"So if we find out who snatched the sparrow—"

"We'll know who pinched the penguin," Natalie said.

I looked at her openmouthed in admiration. "Birdie, you're pretty sharp," I said. "Remind me to start paying you more."

"But Chet, you don't pay me anything."

"Then it should be easy to pay you *more*, shouldn't it?"

Since Charles de Gull and his gang were still our top suspects, we scooted back to the school to catch him at soccer practice. With the big game only a day away, he was probably sweating it up on the field.

I never get tired of being right.

Sure enough, our ragtag team was chasing a black-and-white ball while Coach Stroganoff bellowed. Natalie and I sneaked under the bleachers to spy.

A whistle blew.

One of the team's star forwards, a lithe ferret, trotted off the field for instructions. Charles de Gull and Zibo watched from the bench with a sneer.

"Way to hustle, Mindy!" said Coach Stroganoff. While he ran down the next play, a scary-looking rabbit ambled forward.

"Let's go!" barked the ferret. The bunny hopped to it, wiping off Mindy's sweat, giving her a drink, and spraying her face.

I looked closer. Frankenbunny?

"Check her out," I said to Natalie.

"I'd rather not," she said.

"It's that horrible hopper who was hanging out with Ginger."

"So? Maybe she likes soccer, too."

When the bunny had finished pampering her, Mindy rejoined the field.

De Gull spoke up. "So, *mon* coach," he said, "for ze beeg game, you put me on ze starting team, yes?"

The big groundhog swiveled his head. "I put you on the starting team, no," he growled. "When you play better, you can start."

A heavy storm front blew in across the seagull's face. He muttered to Zibo.

Coach blew his whistle, and play resumed.

I elbowed Natalie. "We're missing something here. It doesn't add up."

"Neither does your math homework, but that never stopped you before."

"What's the deal? We've detected lots of school spirit, but no kidnappers."

"Patience," said Natalie, grooming her wing feathers.

"Easy for you to say. You're not the one facing time in the hoosegow."

"*Hoosegow?*" she said. "Chet, where do you get these words?"

I shrugged. "Same place I get all my best detective ideas: late-night movies."

Practicing patience didn't come easy for a gecko of action like me. The only excitement occurred five minutes later, when Mindy shuffled off the field.

"What's up?" said the coach. "We've got another half hour."

Mindy made a face. "I know, Coach, but... well, I just don't feel like it."

"Oh, really?" asked the groundhog. "What *do* you feel like?"

"Um, doing my science homework. Can I go now?"

Coach Stroganoff's face flushed. "*NO,* you can't go! Get back out there!"

The ferret dragged onto the grass. Her play was erratic. When a ball knocked Mindy down, the coach finally pulled her out and substituted de Gull.

I straightened a crick in my neck. "Natalie, this

stakeout is strictly for sports fans. We're not getting the goods on whoever snatched Bland."

"I guess not," she said, face falling. "I was so sure we'd find some clues."

Climbing out from under the bleachers, I said, "Time for Plan B: We search the school, see if we can get lucky and maybe find us some penguin tracks."

Unfortunately, my luck had taken a three-week vacation to Timbuktu (along with my grades). Our hunt was a total washout. We faced facts and gave up.

There are only so many places you can hide a chubby penguin. And James Bland was in exactly none of them.

As we shuffled home, Natalie asked, "What now, Mr. PI?"

"I'm running out of options. It pains me to say it, but there's only one thing left to do."

"What's that?"

"Household chores," I said. "See you tomorrow, birdie."

10

Countdown to Lockup

The next day began with my back to the wall. Seven hours to locate a penguin, or I'd learn just how pretty I'd look in jail stripes. I needed a lead, a clue—heck, even a miracle would do.

But all I found were dead ends.

Natalie and I tried to dig up Connie Vitus to grill her again. But the sparrow was home with the flu.

I questioned Elise Navidad on the penguin's whereabouts, but the reporter laughed me out of her studio. It seemed my reputation had only gotten worse.

All through the day, the clock ticked mercilessly, counting down my hours of freedom. Come three o'clock, I'd be washed up at Emerson Hicky.

And we're not talking laundry day.

At lunch, Principal Zero passed me on the playground. He lifted an eyebrow as if to ask, *Any results?*

I shook my head—*No luck.*

He held up three fingers. *Three more hours.*

It's a scary thing when you can read your principal's mind.

School spirit bubbled all around me. My classmates were pumped about the big soccer game. But I couldn't muster enough zip to blow up a soggy balloon.

I was kaput, *fini,* down the drain, yesterday's news. I would have turned myself in early, but I didn't want to miss my last recess as a free gecko.

Somehow, my unknown foe had succeeded where some of the worst crooks had failed. I was out of business.

At recess, I slumped on the swing, barely moving. My whole detective career flashed before my eyes. It wasn't pretty.

And it was all over much too soon.

Grabbing the chains, I hung backward. Maybe the world would look better upside down.

Nope.

I found myself face-to-gut with a bird's belly.

"Why aren't you chasing down leads?" said Natalie.

"We're fresh out."

"What happened to Chet Gecko, detective ace?"

"He turned out to be a joker," I mumbled.

Natalie shook the chains. "Snap out of it!"

"Aah!" I lost my grip and sprawled in the sand. "What'd you do that for?"

She clenched her fists. "Because Chet Gecko is no quitter."

"He's not?"

"We've still got an hour and a half, and I won't let you go down without a fight!" (Even if she had to fight me to make sure of it.)

I held up my hands. "All right, all right."

Sheesh. These dizzy dames. A guy can't even whine in peace.

Natalie helped me up. "Let's go over everything once more," she said. "Because we're missing something obvious."

"Okay," I said, wandering onto the playground. "Um...Ginger hired us to protect her sister, who then disappeared with de Gull and his gang."

"But de Gull says he didn't kidnap her," said Natalie.

"Well, duh," I said. "He's a bad guy; he would."

Natalie cocked her head. "But what if he was telling the truth?"

"Sure, and if cows could fly, we'd all have to wear umbrella hats."

"No, really. Maybe they didn't kidnap Connie Vitus."

"So who did?" I skirted a hopscotch game.

Natalie lifted a shoulder. "I don't know..."

I stopped short. "Hey, maybe we're asking the wrong question."

"You mean, Who put the 'ding' in the 'rama lama ding dong'?"

"No," I said. "We've been asking, *Who kidnapped Connie?* Maybe we should be asking, *Where did they keep her?*"

"Now you're cookin', Mr. PI. So where was she?"

I scratched under my hat. "Let's see...Connie said some kind of nest...a nest of crooks?"

"Right," said Natalie. "And where do you find a nest?"

"At the nearest Nest Improvement Store?" I asked.

"Nearer than that." Natalie tilted her head back and gazed up into the branches of a nearby tree.

At last the raisins landed in that bowl of oatmeal I call my brain. "So we've been searching in the wrong place."

"Bingo bongo," said Natalie. "Time to take to the treetops."

I should have known. To find a bird, ask a bird.

11

Wild Wild Nest

Time was running shorter than a principal's patience, so Natalie and I split up. She took one side of the playground, and I covered the other.

I hustled from tree to tree, scuttling up them to peer into high branches, then sliding back down. Although I caught a couple of sixth-grade tree frogs making out (*eew!*), my search was otherwise fruitless.

Shading my eyes, I scouted the skies for my partner. Natalie was patrolling the wild patch of woods just beyond school property.

Suddenly, she swooped into the branches of an oak.

Had she found something? I hotfooted it across the grass. Natalie glided back over the fence and signaled me.

Amanda Reckonwith, the teacher on yard duty, was breaking up a knot of squabbling second graders. She wouldn't like us leaving the school grounds.

But then, she didn't need to know.

Natalie's face shone with excitement.

"What is it?" I asked.

"Come on!" she said. "Slip out, and follow me. It's big!"

With a few easy flaps, Natalie was airborne.

I casually strolled to the fence and eyeballed Ms. Reckonwith. When the teacher's back was turned, I scrambled up and over.

"Hurry!" hissed Natalie from somewhere ahead and above.

Quick as a hummingbird's heartbeat, I dashed between the trees. We had a couple of minutes at most before recess ended.

If we were late, we'd get detention. Of course, if I didn't find Bland, I'd be in the hoosegow. I didn't want to know how I'd serve detention in jail, but I knew my school would find a way.

"Where are you?" I called.

"Up here!" Her voice rang from the oak dead ahead.

I scuttled up its trunk.

A lazy horsefly circled in the still air.

Za-zzip! I shot out my tongue and slurped him down.

Heck, even a PI in a pickle needs a snack.

"Stop feeding your face and get over here," said Natalie from her perch.

Resuming my climb, I soon reached the tree's fork. "All right," I said. "What's all the fuss abou—"

Bonk!

"Ow!" My head hit something solid.

Strange. I could have sworn I had plenty of headroom.

Rubbing my noggin, I looked up. A massive, mud-daubed nest perched just above, disguised by painted leaves and branches to be invisible from below.

I whistled. "A hideout."

"A hidden hideout," said Natalie.

"*Mff!* Ngg mf *gnng!*" said the nest.

I cocked my head. "A talking hideout?"

"No, bug brains, there's someone inside," she said. "Help me find the door."

We swarmed over the crash pad, which seemed almost half the size of my classroom. At the top, we found a hole.

"Here goes nothing," I said, and slid down it feetfirst.

Foomp!

A soft cushion of feathers, sweaters, and musty backpacks broke my fall. Somebody had raided the lost-and-found.

"Okay," I called, and Natalie scooted down after me.

We took a gander at the lair. It had everything the well-appointed hideout should have: mysterious maps and charts; a laptop computer; a small fridge; a scale model of a volcano; a rack of colorful chemicals in tubes; and a chubby penguin, trussed up like a roasted green stinkbug at Christmas.

"Bland!" I cried.

"Mmf," he answered.

12

Bland Date

Hopping to it like grasshoppers on a griddle, Natalie and I untied the penguin and removed his gag. We helped him sit up.

"Thanks awfully, old chums," he said. "Sorry to be a bother."

"A *bother*?" I said. My fists clenched. He'd been so much more than a bother, there wasn't even a word for it. "You ruined my reputation, you almost got me arrested, you . . . you . . ."

Natalie stepped between us. "And he's sorry for it. *Aren't you,* James?"

"Eh?" said the befuddled penguin. "Oh, ever so."

"Then, why the disappearing act, buddy boy? Trying to get me in Dutch?"

Bland's beak fell open. "I should say not. I really was kidnapped."

"By whom?" asked Natalie.

"That dreadful little bird, Ginger Vitus," he said.

The freight train of my brain ran into a mountain of pudding. "Uh, Ginger?"

"The same," said Bland. "We were getting along famously, but then she turned on me, didn't she?"

"She did?" I said.

"Rather. The little minx."

"Sparrow," said Natalie.

"Whatever," said the penguin. "First, she engaged me to find her sister..."

"Don't remind me," I said.

"Then after I did, she lured me up here and kept me—without so much as a crumpet! I say, you don't happen to have any sardine puffs, do you?"

I shook my head. In spite of myself, I felt for the guy. All tied up and nothing to nosh.

"So how *did* you find Connie?" asked Natalie.

"Oh, an anonymous note," said Bland. "It said to look up a certain tree, so I did, didn't I? And there she was, all tied up."

I gaped. "An anonymous note? You found her when I couldn't, just because of a stupid *note*?"

Both Natalie and Bland eyed me warily.

But instead of exploding, I guffawed. "Some detective you are!"

The penguin avoided my eyes. "Uh, well...actually, I'm not."

"What?"

"Not a detective," he said, wincing. "It's a, well...it's a new school, and I thought if I pretended to be something glam, like a PI, then all the kids would jolly well want to be my friend."

Natalie cackled. "You don't know many private eyes, do you?"

"Watch it," I said. "This is a classy job."

"Precisely," said Bland. "And my bluff went smashingly, until I got nicked."

I frowned. "But why did Ginger kidnap you? You did what she asked."

The penguin rubbed his face with a flipper. "Yes, well, I seem to have overheard Ginger and her geek patrol plotting some dodgy scheme."

"They're stealing a dodgeball?" I asked.

"Not the ball," he said. "The scheme—it's dodgy, skeevy, wonky."

"Right." I glanced at Natalie. "Are we speaking the same language?"

Bland blew out a sigh. "They're gonna bring the heat at the big game if we don't bust a move, yo."

"That's all you had to say," I said. "Let's stop that sparrow!"

The class bell jangled.

Uh-oh.

"Hurry!" said Natalie, springing to the short tunnel.

"Right behind you," I said.

We scrambled out onto the top of the nest.

Behind us, James Bland grunted and huffed. "I say, lend a chap a hand?"

Tugging on his flippers, we hauled the penguin up.

"Let's skedaddle," I said, shinnying down the trunk.

Natalie crouched, ready for takeoff.

"Wait!" cried the penguin. "Don't leave me."

"Come with us, you goof," said Natalie. "Climb down."

"Can't climb," he said.

"Then fly," I said.

"But I'm a flightless bird, aren't I!" he wailed.

I stared at him. "Then how the heck did you get up here?"

The penguin blushed. "She lured me with a herring milk shake and a ladder."

"We'll get you down," I said. "Stay put."

Natalie took flight, and I legged it. With any luck, the playground would be empty, and we could slip onto it unnoticed.

Reaching the fence, I saw the last of the kids heading back to class. Perfect.

Up and over I scrambled, landing on the far side

with a *whump*. If Coach Stroganoff knew I got this much exercise willingly, he'd never believe it.

I checked left and right. The coast was clear. Natalie dipped a wing as she sailed past, headed for the buildings.

Pouring on the steam, I lit out across the grass.

"Chet Gecko!" A voice sliced the air like cold steel through warm eggplant.

I skidded to a halt.

Ms. Amanda Reckonwith, snapping turtle, rose from her seat on a low wall. "You, mister, are in big trouble. You left school property."

"But I found James Bland," I said. "He's over there—"

"Oh, I'm sure he is," said the teacher, marching over to me. "And you probably found the Loch Ness Monster, too."

"But I *did* find him," I said. "Bland, I mean, not the monster."

She shoved her beaky nose in my face. "I don't care *what* you were doing. You left school grounds, and rules are rules."

"But I—"

"Shut . . . your . . . trap," she growled. (I had never heard a turtle growl before, and I hope I never do again.) "You've got three days' detention, buster— starting right after school!"

There are two ways to argue with a teacher on yard duty.

Neither one of them works.

Ms. Reckonwith pointed to the buildings. "March!"

What can you do when they've got your number? I marched.

13

Short Detention Span

Back in class, kids stood in front of the room and blathered on and on about their relatives. Family history reports, they called it. My time was better spent brainstorming. Somehow I had to see Principal Zero, rescue Bland, and bust up Ginger's dirty scheme—all before serving detention or landing in jail.

I tried the direct approach.

"Mr. Ratnose," I said, raising my hand, "can I go to the principal's office?"

The lean rat frowned. "No, you may not. Sit still and listen to Waldo."

I tried charm.

"Mr. Ratnose?"

"What?" he said.

"Can I please make one phone call—pretty please with grubworms on top?" I made Bambi eyes at him.

"No," he said. "Now settle down."

I even tried obnoxiousness.

Leaning over my desk and waving like a teacher's pet, I cried, "Ooh, ooh!"

Mr. Ratnose twitched his whiskers. "Chet Gecko," he said, "if you're trying to annoy me so much that I send you to the principal's office, it won't work."

Dang. He was one wise rat.

I fumed, but could do nothing more until class ended.

When the bell rang, I blasted out the door. With a pinch of luck and some fleet feet, I might make the office before the Detention Queen nabbed me.

Bent low, I wove through the after-school crowd. Kids laughed and shouted, trooping down to the field for the soccer game.

At an exposed crossroads, I ducked behind a burly beaver. So far, so good.

Confident in my sneaking skills, I was already deciding what to say to Mr. Zero. Maybe that's why I didn't spot the turtle planted directly in my path.

"You there!" snapped Ms. Reckonwith.

I froze. "Me here?"

"Did you get lost?" She pointed a leathery arm. "Detention hall is that way."

"I, uh, just needed to see the principal first."

Amanda Reckonwith twisted her mouth into a parody of a smile. "If I had a shiny nickel for every time I heard that excuse, I'd have a villa by the sea."

And right then, I wished she was there. "But it's not—" I began.

"Hold your tongue, mister," said the snapping turtle. "And haul your tail into Room Three. Ms. Glick is absent today, so I shall be conducting detention."

Great. The only thing worse than Warden Glick was Warden Reckonwith.

She reached out, seized my shoulders, and spun me around. "Move it."

I trudged toward the booger green door of Room 3. How could I escape my fate? I swiveled, searching for Natalie. But my partner was nowhere near.

Trapped, I entered the room. Four other low-down jailbirds shared my fate. They glanced up as I walked in, then slumped back into their private miseries.

I collapsed on a chair. If I couldn't bust out of there, I'd experience real prison, and detention would seem like a trip to the zoo on a shiny new bicycle.

Ms. Reckonwith blew in and shut the door with a click. She cast an eye over us. "Keep your trap shut and your hands to yourself," she said, "and we'll get along just fine."

The turtle settled behind her desk.

I eyed the window. Kids were still streaming past on their way to the game.

Any minute now, I expected Natalie to spring me. Any minute now.

But the minutes ticked by. No Natalie.

Had my partner run out on me? Or worse, gotten into a jam with Ginger?

It looked like I'd have to bail myself out of this one.

Lucky thing Ms. Reckonwith didn't know me as well as Mr. Ratnose did. I decided to try a technique that often worked for my little sister Pinky.

I raised my hand. "Teacher, can I go to the principal's office?"

"It's *may I?*" she said. "And no, you may not."

"Why?" I asked.

"Because I said so."

"Why?"

"Because I don't want you leaving this room," she snarled.

"Why?"

"Because you might not come back and finish your detention."

"Why?"

She gripped the edge of the desk. "Because you're a shifty little snoop."

"Why?"

"I DON'T KNOW WHY!" shouted Ms. Reckonwith. She scrawled something on her pink pad, stomped down the aisle, and thrust the sheet into my hand. "I've had enough of you. Go straight to Mr. Zero's office and give him this."

"Will do." I got up and walked to the door. "And Ms. Reckonwith?"

"What?"

"Thanks."

14

Ladder Rip

I caught Principal Zero just as he was heading out to the soccer game. The big cat seemed almost disappointed that I'd dug up James Bland. Maybe he'd been looking forward to a gecko-free year.

Still, Mr. Zero gave me the green light to go and fetch the penguin.

"But if this turns out to be one of your lies," he said, "I'll send you to jail in a red-hot jiffy."

"Could I take a taxi instead?" I asked.

"Gecko!"

Quick like a bunny, I hippety-hopped out to the playground fence. Natalie was waiting with the mongoose custodian Maureen DeBree and a ladder.

"Took you long enough," she said. Natalie shifted on her fence-top perch.

"I had to bust out of detention all on my own," I said, scrambling up the ladder to join her.

Maureen DeBree stuck her furry fingers in her ears. "I'm not hearing this."

Natalie lifted a shoulder. "I couldn't pull a fast one on Ms. Reckonwith," she said. "She's my teacher."

The three of us wrestled the ladder up and over. "But it's okay for me to pull a fast one?" I said.

"It's what you do," said Natalie.

Couldn't argue with that.

Ms. DeBree waited on the school side of the fence. "You private eyeballs better bring back my ladder in one piece, eh?"

"We won't do you rung," said Natalie.

The mongoose grunted. "I wait right here."

Natalie and I hoisted the ladder and lugged it through the trees.

"I hope James is still there," she said.

"He better be," I said. "'Cause if something's happened to him, I'm gonna kill him."

We staggered up to the oak tree. No sign of the wannabe detective.

"Bland!" I called. "Where are you?"

"Olly, olly, oxen free!" cried Natalie.

I glanced at her. "You know, I've always wondered

about that. Does it mean that the oxen don't cost anything?"

"Or is it telling some guy named Olly that his livestock has escaped?"

"I say, chums," came a voice from the tree fork. "You are going to rescue me by teatime, aren't you? I'm a bit peckish."

"That seems only right for a bird," I said.

We wrangled the ladder up against the trunk, and with Natalie's help, the penguin made his way down it.

I was helpful and supportive. Of course, it would've taken a stronger gecko than me not to crack up when Bland missed the last four rungs and landed—*boomf!*—on his bubble butt.

"Ooh!" he said, struggling to his feet. "Thanks awfully. I say, I'm absolutely famished. Don't suppose either of you has the odd bonito biscuit?"

"Not even the even one," I said. "We've gotta get you to the game, pronto."

His eyes brightened. "And settle Ginger's hash?"

"Buddy," I said. "Can't you think of anything else but food?"

"Look who's talking," said Natalie. "Now, let's go!"

We dragged the ladder back through the woods and propped it against the fence where Maureen DeBree waited.

"You found the missing kid," she said. "Maybe you really *is* one hotshot detective, eh?"

"All in a day's work, sister. Give us a hand?"

A soft *clap-clap-clap* came from Ms. DeBree's side of the fence.

I shook my head. Custodian humor.

With the mongoose's help, we hustled penguin, ladder, and ourselves back over onto school property. A distant cheer floated from the playing field.

"What time is it?" I asked the janitor.

She checked her watch. "Almost three o'clock."

"Come on!" I said. "Time to give that sparrow her just deserts!"

"*Mmm,* dessert," murmured Bland.

I charged across the playground, Natalie flapping just overhead. But we hadn't gone far when she said, "Chet, wait."

"For what?"

"James."

Slowing, I glanced back. The penguin waddled along on his stubby legs, sluggish as a Sunday in August.

"Hurry!" I cried.

"This is as hurry-ish as I get," said Bland. "Penguins aren't built for speed."

My teeth clenched. The big butterball was costing us time. But I couldn't get off the hook without him.

I jogged back. What a time to get caught without my skateboard.

Skateboard? *Hmm.*

Eyeballing the slope of the lawn, I asked, "Ever done any sledding, Bland?"

His forehead creased. "Well...on the snow? Certainly, old bean."

"Try grass, old sprout," I said.

"Well, all right," said Bland. "But I don't suppose it's very tasty."

When he bent to nibble the lawn, I gave him a
boot in his penguin booty.

"Oof!" Bland belly flopped onto the lawn.

I hopped onto his back like a flea at a dog show,
kicked once, twice with my foot, and away we slid.

"Oi!" said James Bland.

"Ride 'em, Gecko!" called Natalie from above.

Faster and faster we glided, pouring on steam as
the slope increased. I whooped and guided him
around some bushes. "Go, Bland, go!"

We just might make it after all, I thought.

A trash can loomed dead ahead.

Or not.

15

Soccer Blew

"**W**atch out for the—" cried Bland.

"Yikes!" I grabbed his fins and steered hard right.

Ffssssh! We brushed past on edge, toppling the can and spilling its trash.

"Ms. DeBree won't like that," cried Natalie.

"Never mind her," I said, wrestling for control of the speeding penguin. "Just watch for obstacles."

My Bland-sled spun a 360, nearly dumping me before I could get us back on track.

"Easy on the—*oof!*—old tum-tum," he said.

Luckily for the penguin, his old tum-tum was well padded. But he'd still have a heckuva belly burn.

Flapping just overhead, Natalie said, "This reminds me of a song."

"'The Electric Slide'?" I asked.

"Nope." She sang, "Dashing through the snow, in a one-penguin open sleigh . . . Through the school we go, laughing all the—*stairs!*"

I glanced up. "Huh? *Stairs* doesn't rhyme with *sleigh.*"

"No, Chet . . ."

"*Stairs!*" cried Natalie and Bland together.

We crested a rise, and then I saw it: The grass ended in a flight of stairs.

My body tensed. No way to stop in time.

"Hang on!" I cried, clutching the penguin's flippers in a death grip.

"AAAHHHH!" cried James Bland.

And we were airborne.

Hang time is slow-mo time. I could see past the stairs to the gym and the soccer field beyond. I could read the scoreboard: PETSADENA 3, EMERSON HICKY 0. In fact, I even had the chance to regret my bogus science report on land sharks.

But hang time doesn't last.

The penguin's body hit with a *whump!* As we jounced down the steps, Bland's cry turned to "AH-uh-AH-uh-AH!"

Ka-fomp!

We collapsed in a detective dog pile at the foot of the stairs.

I lay still. The world had turned dark, suffocating, and as cramped as a hermit crab's closet. I struggled, but couldn't move. Had the fall paralyzed me?

"Mmf!" I cried.

Something tugged on my leg. Then the world rolled away and I could breathe again.

"Chet, are you okay?" asked Natalie.

I grinned weakly. "As okay as anyone smushed by a penguin butt could be."

She helped me to my feet.

"Let's go bust a sparrow," I said. "Coming, James?"

Bland levered himself up. "Can't pack it in just yet. Let's carry on."

Supporting each other, we staggered past a low fence and out to the field. The cheers seemed especially loud and the uniforms especially bright. Everything spun with an off-key giddiness, like a carnival in Munchkin Land.

"Sure you're okay?" said Natalie as I weaved.

"Never better," I said. "Where's Mr. Zero?"

Natalie's sharp eyes spotted our principal in the front row of bleachers. I waved to the hefty tomcat and pointed at Bland.

Principal Zero scowled, nodded grudgingly, and twitched an ear. That was as close to an apology as the big guy ever got.

I turned to the game. The field was utter chaos—kids in silver jerseys and golden jerseys butting and tripping one another, while adults screamed from the sidelines. Madness reigned.

"We're too late!" I cried. "Ginger's pulled off her plan."

Natalie lifted an eyebrow. "This is what our soccer games usually look like."

"Oh," I said. "I really must get out more often."

She turned to James Bland. "So, what's Ginger's plan?"

The plump penguin smiled weakly. "I don't actually, er, know, do I?"

"You don't?" I said, scanning for the sparrow. "Well, that's just swell."

"Over there, Chet," said Natalie.

Ginger Vitus, Frankenbunny, and a gawky box turtle stood by the benches on our side, holding towels and spray bottles. Coach Stroganoff called a time-out, and three Emerson Hicky players jogged off-field.

"Look alive, you geeks!" shouted one of the players. Ginger and her nerd pals bustled over, wiped off the athletes' sweat, and spritzed them.

"Pretty sinister," I said. "And for this I nearly got thrown in the slammer?"

"Let's have a look-see, shall we?" said Bland.

As we approached, the coach was arguing with Charles de Gull.

"I don't care if you're the greatest player since Jacques Le Strappe," said Coach Stroganoff. "You go in when I say you go."

"But ze team, she eez losing!" squawked the gull.

"Siddown," barked the groundhog.

Charles de Gull mumbled, casting black looks at Ginger. She pretended not to notice.

Coach gave some last orders to the three players, a beefy duck and two raccoons, then clapped his paws. "Let's play some ball!" he yelled.

The three jocks ran back onto the field, shaking their heads and wobbling a little. Whistles shrilled, and the game resumed.

I stopped behind Ginger. "Well, if it isn't the evil birdbrain herself."

The sparrow jumped. Frankenbunny and the turtle gasped.

"Wh-what are you doing here?" said Ginger.

"I've come to clip your wings, upset your apple-cart, spike your scheme."

Several expressions chased each other across her face. Ginger settled on innocent. "What scheme?"

"I say, Chet," said James Bland.

"Not now, ace." I eyed the sparrow. "What do you take me for?"

"A has-been," she said.

"You didn't shoot down my rep just for yuks."

"Uh, Chet?" said Natalie.

"Later. You didn't snatch Bland and stash him in your nest for nothing."

Ginger pouted. "I don't know what you're, uh, talking about."

"Chet, *look!*" cried Natalie.

"What is it?" I followed her gaze.

Out on the field, Emerson Hicky's athletes were tripping over their own feet like dodo birds at a disco. One of the raccoons slipped and did a face-plant, right into the grass. The duck stumbled into Mindy, knocking the ball loose.

A triumphant Petsadena player booted it in for a goal.

"Yeah, so?" I said. "Our jocks are duds."

Natalie shook her head. "Something's nutty."

"Or nerdy." Charles de Gull spat from the bench.

"Come again?" I said.

Ginger shot the gull a dark look of her own. "Charles . . ."

"No!" he spat. "You promise eef I 'elp you fake Connie's kidnapping, I would play. But I am still warming ze bench."

"That's not *my* fault," said the sparrow.

"Hah," said de Gull. "Enough lies. Zees eez her plan: She turn ze team into geeks, and we lose."

I blinked. "What? How?"

"Simple, smart guy," snarled Ginger. "With nerd spray."

And she spritzed a double squirt of her bottle—right into my face.

16

A Nerd's-Eye View

"*Aaugh!*" I wiped my streaming eyes on my sleeve.

By the time my vision cleared, Ginger's friends had scattered, and the sparrow herself had taken to the skies.

"Get her, Natalie!" I shouted.

"I'm on it!" she said, flapping in pursuit.

I dashed onto the field, bumping bodies, trying to keep the sparrow in sight.

"Hey, watch it!" snarled a chuckwalla in Petsadena silver.

"Where's your jersey?" asked a weasel.

"Next to my york," I said. (But I doubted they got the joke.)

Up above, Natalie overtook Ginger, wheeling to force her to turn.

A strange tingle numbed my face. I shook my head, and zigzagged after the sparrow.

Strange thoughts clouded my mind. Fractions and two-digit multiplication, the Treaty of West Kalamazoo, the difference between igneous and sedimentary rocks—all made a kind of beautiful sense.

An odd feeling crept over me. I wanted to . . . *study?*

"Unh!" I smashed into a hefty toad and stumbled back. Pain cleared my head. My aim returned.

Get Ginger.

Glancing up at her, I thought, *as my study partner.*

I bit the inside of my cheek. "No, dummy. Stop her!"

"Huh?" said a nearby otter.

Fighting the urge to sit down and crack a book, I hauled after the sparrow, who was headed toward Petsadena's goal. I was gaining—only yards to go.

My legs pumped like pistons. I reached for Ginger's dangling claws.

Just another few inches . . .

"Gecko, think fast!" someone called.

As my foot swept forward, it met something hard and rubbery.

Poomf!

I booted the soccer ball just as my hand glommed on to Ginger's leg.

"Gotcha!"

For a few brief moments, I was airborne. The crowd cheered.

"Let go!" she cried, kicking with her free leg. "We'll crash!"

Ginger dipped. I looked down in time to see the goalie's wide eyes.

Whoomp!

We scooped him up like a feather-and-scale cyclone.

Foomp! The three of us hit the goal net.

All was a crazy goulash of legs and tails, arms and elbows, until the referees got us untangled.

"Spectacular goal, Gecko." Coach Stroganoff chuckled, looking me up and down. "Have you ever considered soccer?"

A voice in my head said, *Yeah, I consider it a total waste of time,* but I guessed that was just the nerd juice talking.

"Think how good he'd be if he actually practiced," said Natalie.

James Bland showed up with Mr. Zero in tow. Ginger wilted under the principal's stare, like dandelion salad in a microwave oven.

"Missy, you've got a lot of explaining to do," he growled.

The sparrow hung her head. "I, uh, just wanted to show them how it feels to be a geek like me," she whimpered. "I didn't want to hurt anyone."

Mr. Zero's tail twitched. "You consider kidnapping not hurting anyone?"

"I guess it got a little, uh, out of hand?"

"I'd jolly well say so," Bland sputtered. "These blighters had me in a freezing-cold dungeon lined with spikes, ringed round by a piranha-infested moat. Why, Chet and Natalie had to fight past rabid wolverines to—"

"Is that true, Gecko?" asked Coach Stroganoff, arching a furry eyebrow.

I spread my hands. "Would an ace PI tell a lie?"

The penguin beamed a surprised thank-you. Mr. Zero harrumphed.

He took Ginger by a wing. "You and your little friends will join me in my office now," he said. "A couple of boys in blue are dying to meet you."

The massive cat collected Frankenbunny and the turtle, and he led the three nerds away. I suspected that the spanking machine would be working overtime.

"I hope he throws the book at that lot," said James Bland.

"Oh, I dunno," I said. "They're not really *that* evil . . ."

Natalie tugged on the skin of my cheek.

"Hey, easy on the merchandise," I said.

"Just checking that you're not some impostor wearing a Chet Gecko costume," she said. "I could have sworn my partner was ready to fricassee whoever wrecked his reputation."

I pushed back my hat and scratched my head. "Well, I . . . guess I know how Ginger feels, that's all."

"How she *feels*?" said Natalie. "Who-*ee*! You must have gotten a double dose of that nerd spray."

The penguin flung a flipper over our shoulders. "I say, old chums, as long as we're here, shall we find some nibbles and watch the game?"

I looked from them to the teams on the field, and felt a warm buzz.

"Actually," I said. "I've got something important to do—something I've been needing to do for a long time."

"Thank-yous?" said Natalie.

"Revenge?" asked Bland.

"Homework," I said. "See you tomorrow."

17

Swing Cleaning

By the next day, the effects of the nerd spray had evaporated like a bully's bluff in the principal's office. I had to struggle through morning lessons using the same wits I was born with.

Yes, it was that bad.

Still, I got to savor Mr. Ratnose's expression when my math homework earned a perfect score. He hadn't looked like that since someone moved his favorite cheese.

By recess, the details of Ginger's scheme had spread throughout the school. Apparently, she and her chemistry club pals had developed the spray as an experiment in boosting intelligence.

When they discovered that clumsiness came as a side effect, Ginger hatched her plan to take down the jocks who had always mocked them. She faked her sister's kidnapping to trash my reputation and put me on ice.

Then, when I still came up swinging, she framed me for Bland's disappearance. Twisted? Yes. But flattering, too. All that plotting, just to get rid of little ol' me.

At recess, Natalie and I were enjoying some quality time on the swings.

"One thing I don't understand," she said.

"Why, if you spill spot remover on a dog, he doesn't disappear?"

"No," she said. "Why, if the nerd spray was supposed to make kids klutzy, you didn't act any klutzier than usual."

I leaned back and pulled on the chains as the swing rushed forward. "Maybe I'm invulnerable. Like Superman."

Natalie cackled. "Right. Or maybe you can't be any klutzier than you already are."

I swung in silence for a while, savoring that glow that comes from wrapping up a case. I'd get her back, of course, but not just yet.

"You know," I said, "maybe it's just the after-effects of the nerd spray, but I've been thinking…"

"Careful, it's tricky the first time out."

"Ha, ha," I said. "Seriously. I feel like I understand Ginger a little more than the usual bad guys we've busted."

Natalie whooshed backward on the swing. "Does this mean you're becoming a nerd?"

"Fat chance. But Grandma Gecko always said, before you criticize someone, you should walk a mile in their shoes."

Her eyebrows lifted. "So you'll know how they feel inside?"

"No," I said. "So that when you criticize them, you'll be a mile away *and* you'll have their shoes."

Natalie shook her head in admiration. "Well, the nerd spray may have worn off, but you've hung on to a certain kind of smarts."

"Yeah?" I said.

"The Chet Gecko kind: smart-aleck smarts."

I saluted her as the swing whooshed me forward. "And that's the best kind, birdie."

**Look for more mysteries from
the Tattered Casebook of Chet Gecko
in hardcover and paperback**

Case #1 *The Chameleon Wore Chartreuse*

Some cases start rough, some cases start easy. This one started with a dame. (That's what we private eyes call a girl.) She was cute and green and scaly. She looked like trouble and smelled like ... grasshoppers.

Shirley Chameleon came to me when her little brother, Billy, turned up missing. (I suspect she also came to spread cooties, but that's another story.) She turned on the tears. She promised me some stinkbug pie. I said I'd find the brat.

But when his trail led to a certain stinky-breathed, bad-tempered, jumbo-sized Gila monster, I thought I'd bitten off more than I could chew. Worse, I had to chew fast: If I didn't find Billy in time, it would be bye-bye, stinkbug pie.

Case #2 *The Mystery of Mr. Nice*

How would you know if some criminal mastermind tried to impersonate your principal? My first clue: He was nice to me.

This fiend tried everything—flattery, friendship, food—but he still couldn't keep me off the case. Natalie and I followed a trail of clues as thin as the cheese on a cafeteria hamburger. And we found a ring of corruption that went from the janitor right up to Mr. Big.

In the nick of time, we rescued Principal Zero and busted up the PTA meeting, putting a stop to the evil genius. And what thanks did we get? Just the usual. A cold handshake and a warm soda.

But that's all in a day's work for a private eye.

Case #3 *Farewell, My Lunchbag*

If danger is my business, then dinner is my passion. I'll take any case if the pay is right. And what pay could be better than Mothloaf Surprise?

At least that's what I thought. But in this particular case, I bit off more than I could chew.

Cafeteria lady Mrs. Bagoong hired me to track down whoever was stealing her food supplies. The long, slimy trail led too close to my own backyard for comfort.

And much, much too close to the very scary Jimmy "King" Cobra. Without the help of Natalie Attired and our school janitor, Maureen DeBree, I would've been gecko sushi.

Case #4 *The Big Nap*

My grades were lower than a salamander's slippers, and my bank account was trying to crawl under a duck's belly. So why did I take a case that didn't pay anything?

Put it this way: Would *you* stand by and watch some

evil power turn *your* classmates into hypnotized zombies? (If that wasn't just what normally happened to them in math class, I mean.)

My investigations revealed a plot meaner than a roomful of rhinos with diaper rash.

Someone at Emerson Hicky was using a sinister video game to put more and more students into la-la-land. And it was up to me to stop it, pronto—before that someone caught up with me, and I found myself taking the Big Nap.

Case #5 *The Hamster of the Baskervilles*

Elementary school is a wild place. But this was ridiculous.

Someone—or some*thing*—was tearing up Emerson Hicky. Classrooms were trashed. Walls were gnawed. Mysterious tunnels riddled the playground like worm chunks in a pan of earthworm lasagna.

But nobody could spot the culprit, let alone catch him.

I don't believe in the supernatural. My idea of voodoo is my mom's cockroach-ripple ice cream.

Then, a teacher reported seeing a monster on full-moon night, and I got the call.

At the end of a twisted trail of clues, I had to answer the burning question: Was it a vicious, supernatural were-hamster on the loose, or just another Science Fair project gone wrong?

Case #6 *This Gum for Hire*

Never thought I'd see the day when one of my worst enemies would hire me for a case. Herman the Gila Monster was a sixth-grade hoodlum with a first-rate left hook. He told me someone was disappearing the football team, and he had to put a stop to it. *Big whoop.*

He told me he was being blamed for the kidnappings, and he had to clear his name. *Boo hoo.*

Then he said that I could either take the case and earn a nice reward, or have my face rearranged like a bargain-basement Picasso painted by a spastic chimp.

I took the case.

But before I could find the kidnapper, I had to go undercover. And that meant facing something that scared me worse than a chorus line of criminals in steel-toed boots: P.E. class.

Case #7 *The Malted Falcon*

It was tall, dark, and chocolatey—the stuff dreams are made of. It was a treat so titanic that nobody had been able to finish one single-handedly (or even single-mouthedly). It was the Malted Falcon.

How far would you go for the ultimate dessert? Somebody went too far, and that's where I came in.

The local sweets shop held a contest. The prize: a year's supply of free Malted Falcons. Some lucky kid scored the winning ticket. She brought it to school for show-and-tell.

But after she showed it, somebody swiped it. And no one would tell where it went.

Following a strong hunch and an even stronger sweet tooth, I tracked the ticket through a web of lies more tangled than a rattlesnake doing the rumba. But the time to claim the prize was fast approaching. Would the villain get the sweet treat—or his just desserts?

Case #8 *Trouble Is My Beeswax*

Okay, I confess. When test time rolls around, I'm as tempted as the next lizard to let my eyeballs do the walking . . . to my neighbor's paper.

But Mrs. Gecko didn't raise no cheaters. (Some language manglers, perhaps.) So when a routine investigation uncovered a test-cheating ring at Emerson Hicky, I gave myself a new case: Put the cheaters out of business.

Easier said than done. Those double-dealers were slicker than a frog's fanny and twice as slimy.

Oh, and there was one other small problem: The finger of suspicion pointed to two dames. The ringleader was either the glamorous Lacey Vail, or my own classmate Shirley Chameleon.

Sheesh. The only thing I hate worse than an empty Pillbug Crunch wrapper is a case full of dizzy dames.

Case #9 *Give My Regrets to Broadway*

Some things you can't escape, however hard you try—like dentist appointments, visits with strange-smelling relatives, and being in the fourth-grade play. I had always left the acting to my smart-aleck pal, Natalie, but then one day it was my turn in the spotlight.

Stage fright? Me? You're talking about a gecko who has laughed at danger, chuckled at catastrophe, and sneezed at sinister plots.

I was terrified.

Not because of the acting, mind you. The script called for me to share a major lip-lock with Shirley Chameleon—Cootie Queen of the Universe!

And while I was trying to avoid that trap, a simple missing persons case took a turn for the worse—right into the middle of my play. Would opening night spell curtains for my client? And, more important, would someone invent a cure for cooties? But no matter—whatever happens, the sleuth must go on.

Case #10 *Murder, My Tweet*

Some things at school you can count on. Pop quizzes always pop up just after you've spent your study time studying comics. Chef's Surprise is always a surprise, but never a good one. And no matter how much you learn today, they always make you come back tomorrow.

But sometimes, Emerson Hicky amazes you. And just like finding a killer bee in a box of Earwig Puffs, you're left shocked, stung, and discombobulated.

Foul play struck at my school; that's nothing new. But then the finger of suspicion pointed straight at my favorite fowl: Natalie Attired. Framed as a blackmailer, my partner was booted out of Emerson Hicky quicker than a hoptoad on a hot plate.

I tackled the case for free. Mess with my partner, mess with me.

Then things took a turn for the worse. Just when I thought I might clear her name, Natalie disappeared. And worse still, she left behind one clue: a reddish smear that looked kinda like the jelly from a beetle-jelly sandwich but raised an ugly question: Was it murder, or something serious?

Case #11 *The Possum Always Rings Twice*

In my time, I've tackled cases stickier than a spider's handshake and harder than three-year-old boll weevil taffy. But nothing compares to the job that landed me knee-deep in school politics.

What seemed like a straightforward case of extortion during Emerson Hicky's student-council election ended up taking more twists and turns than an anaconda's lunch. It became a battle royal for control of the school. (Not that I necessarily believe school is worth fighting for, but a gecko's gotta do *something* with his days.)

In the end, my politicking landed me in one of the tightest spots I've ever encountered. Was I savvy enough to escape with my skin? Let me put it this way: Just like a politician, this is one private eye who always shoots from the lip.